Gold Fever

By Jordan Avery

On a humid summer day, Dad and Pop took the kids for a walk.

They all put on their runners and sunhats.

“Put jackets in your backpacks, too,” said Pop. “It might rain.”

Pop was right.

As they left the bush, it started to rain!

They pulled on their jackets and waited under the trees until the rain stopped.

“It’s lucky we listened to you, Pop!” Devon said.

It only rained for a moment, and then the sun came out.

Mabel spotted a rainbow.

"Look!" she called.

“Do you know the legend about the end of the rainbow?” Mabel asked.

“Yes!” said Devon. “It has a magic pot of gold!”

“Let’s go and find it,” said Mabel. “I’ll fill my backpack full of gold!”

“I wish I had brought my wagon!” said Devon.

All of a sudden, the kids stopped walking.

"We are almost there!" said Devon. "The end of the rainbow is just beyond those trees."

But the trees were on the other side of a river!

“We cannot cross this river!” cried Mabel.

They crossed the river and made it to the trees.

But the end of the rainbow was not there!

You can never locate the rainbow's end.
That is the problem with gold fever.

Mabel and Devon were sad that they did not find any gold.

“The kids learned a hard lesson about gold fever!” said Dad.

I would have used my gold to get a pony.
I would have got some kittens with my gold.

CHECKING FOR MEANING

1. Why did Pop tell the kids to put jackets in their backpacks? *(Literal)*
2. How did the family get across the river? *(Literal)*
3. Did Dad and Pop think the kids would find the gold? How do you know? *(Inferential)*
4. Why do you think Dad and Pop let Mabel and Devon chase the rainbow, even though they knew they would not find the end? *(Evaluative)*

EXTENDING VOCABULARY

humid	What does it feel like when the weather is humid? Does it get humid where you live?
rainbow	Read the word *rainbow*. How many syllables does it have? What two words make up the word *rainbow*? How do the meanings of these words relate to the meaning of *rainbow*?
fever	When do you normally have a fever? Did Mabel and Devon actually have a fever? Why did Dad say that they had *gold fever*?

MOVING BEYOND THE TEXT

1. Have you ever seen a rainbow? What is the weather usually like before a rainbow appears?
2. What might you put in a backpack before going for a bushwalk?
3. If you found gold at the end of a rainbow, what would you do with it?
4. A legend is a traditional story from the past that may or may not be true. What other legends have you heard?

TIME TO WRITE

Imagine you found a pot of gold at the end of a rainbow. How did you feel when you found it? What would you use the gold for?